THE STAR YOU ARE

Marisa Chenault-Dankwa

To order additional copies of this book, contact:
Xlibris
844-714-8691
www.Xlibris.com
Orders@Xlibris.com

ISBN: Softcover   978-1-6698-4442-6
        EBook   978-1-6698-4441-9

Print information available on the last page

Rev. date: 12/06/2022

Inside your chest burns a light.

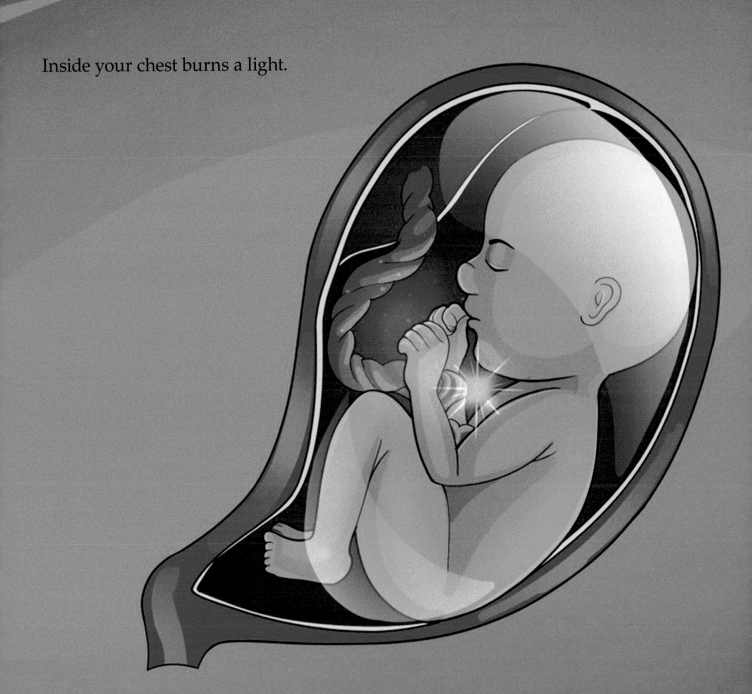

You are a magnificent sight to see.

You are a star. Before you were born into a material body you were an invisible body of gases. Those gases formed into matter. A soul once it entered earths' atmosphere.

You were in two places at one time. You were within mommy. When dawn came through you glowed bright above mommy and daddy. You manifested in human form. The universe wrapped in one. After you were born. You still can be seen in two places at one time. You reign above as higher self. Below you live to experience your lower self. Choosing wisely your path. You must become one with your higher self.

Chapter 2

Your Nature Tailored Purpose

You are extremely vibrant, efficient and energetic. You are flawless, flawless. Like planet earth's gravitational pull. You are here for a purpose. You are connected to all that is natural. You are very important to the universe. Everyone is important. The star you were above shining bright is the same star you are now. You are meant to shine in your human form as well. Your birth says so. With the feminine energy and Masculine working together continuously within you creating a beautiful universe. It is you who in balance and much appreciation for both allow that beauty to shine outside. You traveled a long way to become that energy full of life. You have acquired those lessons along the way. If you start learning things, pressing buttons and offering to help, examine yourself carefully. Your inner sight alerts you that those tasks are very important. Look closely at how excited you are.

Chapter 3

The 12 Lil Star Friends Let's Meet the Various Aspects of Self!

1st Aries

March 21-April 19

Lil Aries is the first sign of Zodiac "its polarity is positive

Cardinal fire over planet mars the human body's head and adrenal glands. Life purpose is to be the first and lead the way, breaking new ground. Aries love to get the action started with youthful zest"!

2nd Taurus

April 20-May 21

Lil Taurus is the second sign of Zodiac" its polarity Negative fixed earth reserved, grounded, and against change ruling over the planet Venus. The human body Neck and throat. Life purpose is to build something of lasting value. More connected to physical reality and the movements of nature".

3rd Gemini

May 22- June 21

Lil Gemini is the third sign of Zodiac, "its polarity is positive Mutable Air ruling Mercury. Human body parts Arms, hands and lungs. Life purpose is in search of "twin" with emphasis on Communication, learning and ideas".

4th **Cancer**

June 22- July 22

Lil Cancer is the fourth sign of Zodiac polarity is negative cardinal water ruling over planet moon. Parts of human body breasts and stomach. Life purpose is to find your tribe and become caretaker in it.

5th Leo

July 23- August 22

Lil Leo the lion is the fifth sign of the Zodiac. "Polarity is positive fixed fire element ruling planet sun parts of human body Heart and Spine. Life purpose is to develop your creative brilliance and become center of attention".

6th Virgo

August 23- September 22

Lil Virgo it is the sixth sign of Zodiac.

Polarity is Negative mutable earth ruling Mercury. Part of the human body Digestive system. Life purpose focus on the craft you love. Being proactive and playing a huge part of a team makes you satisfied.

7th Libra

September 23-October 22

Lil Libra scales of balance the seventh sign of Zodiac. Polarity positive Cardinal air. Ruling Venus. Part of human body Kidneys. Life purpose bring to light and promote civilized living. You find inner balance through developing your poise and grace within yourself.

8th Scorpio

October 23-November 21

Lil Scorpio is the eighth sign of Zodiac. Polarity Negative fixed water ruling Mars and Pluto parts of the human body Reproductive organ and eliminators system. Purpose in life to develop resilience beating odds.

9th Sagittarius

November 22- December 21

Lil Sagittarius is the ninth sign of Zodiac. Polarity is positive mutable Fire ruling over Jupiter. Human body parts Hips and thighs.

Life purpose is to explore, discover and set yourself free on adventures. Soul searching is a must!!

10th Capricorn

December 22- January 19

Lil Capricorn is the tenth sign of Zodiac. "Polarity is Negative Cardinal Earth ruling over Saturn. Human body parts Knees, teeth, bones, and skin. Life purpose develop self-reliance, taking responsibility for both self and others. Focused"!!

11th Aquarius

January 20- February 18

Lil Aquarius is the eleventh sign of Zodiac. "Polarity is Negative Cardinal Earth ruling planet Saturn and Uranus. Human body parts Shins and ankles. Life purpose is to find your place within the group while at the same time asserting your own unique vision".

12th Pisces

February 19- March 20

Lil Pisces is the 12th sign of Zodiac. "Polarity Negative mutable water ruling planet Jupiter and Neptune. Human body parts feet. Life Purpose service to a higher principle. A journey they may require a sacrifice of personal desires. Imagination is key to your life".

Chapter 4

Emotions

Sometimes we tend to allow our emotions to get the best of us.

It isn't good to allow emotions to overrun you.

Think by sitting quietly within those uncomfortable feelings and meditate.

It will allow you to better handle your situations.

When you were a baby crying that was how you communicated your needs.

Now you can talk and express those needs properly.

Chapter 5

Thinking of Others Making Right Choices

We are not on an island alone.

We have others who are like us to consider.

The planets all move together amongst each other on various paths without colliding causing destruction.

We can do the same by sharing, caring and being friendly by helping those in need. This starts at home with mom, dad and siblings.

Rising high means taking the thinking from just the body alone and meditating and taking it to thoughts, which are in the head to help aid you in making well balanced decisions in life and flying within the air of clarity where your soul lives.

Chapter 6

"7 Principles of Your Nature" (Maat) Meaning Balance

These are cultivated energies that naturally reside within you. Words that are formulated from the fabrics of the universe from which you were formed.

1. Truth

2. Justice

3. Harmony

4. Balance

5. Order

6. Reciprocity

7. Propriety

Beware of the illusions which haunt the human condition and interferes through its mental influences.

Chapter 7

"You are Energy"

Energy can't be destroyed

Energy is masculine or Feminine you were made into

A physical form of masculine (concrete/material)

positive and the negative feminine energy (Spiritual/air)

They work together in opposition of each other

The masculine energy moves clockwise

The feminine energy moves counterclockwise

Chapter 8

"Making Great Choices"

You must make the right choices in your life.

The right choices place you on your right path.

The right choices put you in an upward motion.

The right choices will allow you to ascend and transcend pass

The level of this human experience.

Always Keep your Energy High.

Chapter 9

"Taking Care of Self"

Through taking care of self, you take care of others and the planet

It is all connected to the great choices.

The choices that lead you on your path.

Brushing your teeth

Brushing your hair

Getting well needed rest.

Eating whole fresh foods

Keeping yourself clean free from sickness and harmful low energies

Chapter 10

"Respecting Self"

Respecting your self

By not allowing anything to harm your Innocent aura and taking you from your high energy path towards great innovations.

36

The left brain is masculine logic dealing with concrete more of doing seeing is believing dealing with the lower self/ realms. The right brain feminine intuitive dealing with creativity/ imagination it's all about unseen or unnoticed things. You are dealing with the higher self/realms.

We are to utilize our whole brain. Both Intuition and Logic to be winners in all our experiences within this life.

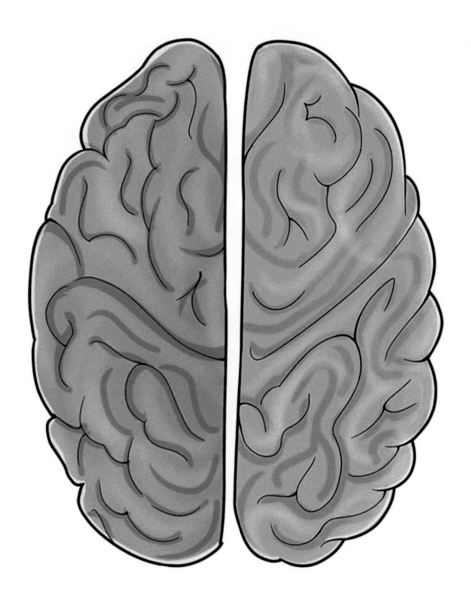

Chapter 11

What is your Totem? Which animal Virtue are you Representing?

Elephant- signifies strength, royalty, patience, wisdom, longevity

Lion- Royalty, conquest, valor, pride, wisdom, authority, courage, and protection

Alligator- Fierce workers, strive for success and abundance while remaining true

Hippopotamus- problem solving, confidence, self-reliance and strength

Zebra- Represents your ability to see situations differently for problem solving and balance.

"God is in the mind, the mind in
the soul, the soul in the matter,
all things by Eternity"
By: Thoth

Not the end
Only the beginning

Printed in the United States
by Baker & Taylor Publisher Services